ADVENTURES AT ASH

SURPRISES

by Lucy Kincaid

CONTENTS

Illustrated by Eric Kincaid

BRIMAX BOOKS•CAMBRIDGE•ENGLAND

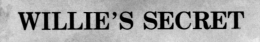

WILLIE'S SECRET

The birds were only just awake and the early morning sun was only just beginning to glint through the trees when the front door of Ash Lodge opened, very, very quietly, and Willie Mole stepped outside. He trotted quickly down the lane towards the post box.

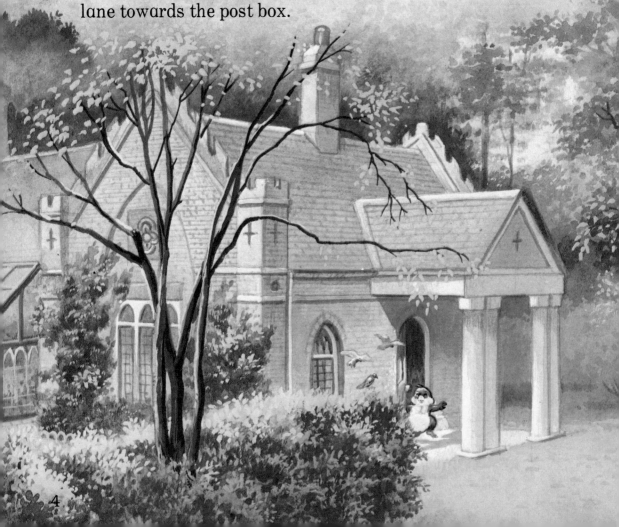

The postman didn't deliver letters to the door of Ash Lodge. He left them in a box at the end of the lane and Willie was expecting a reply to a letter he had written.

"It's come . . . it's come," he whispered excitedly as he lifted a long, narrow parcel from the post box.

5

He had hoped to sneak back indoors before anyone else was up, but he was too late. Basil was standing at the front door taking in the fresh morning air. Willie gasped and ran round to the back door. He couldn't sneak in that way either. Dewy was in the kitchen getting breakfast. He stood quite still and tried not to panic. What could he say about the parcel? One of them was sure to ask what was in it. Before he could make up his mind what to do Dewy looked up and saw him. Dewy was so surprised to see Willie in the garden, when he had supposed him to be asleep in bed, that he dropped the egg he was supposed to be breaking into the frying pan, onto the floor instead. There was barely time to push the parcel into a hiding place before Dewy flung open the kitchen window and demanded to know what Willie meant by giving him such a fright.

Willie stuck his nose in the air.

"I suppose I can go for an early morning walk if I want to," he said, and marched into the kitchen. "What's for breakfast? I'm hungry. I hope you're not going to give me THAT egg. I like my yolks UNbroken."

"Perhaps he's not feeling very well," said Basil.

"Oh, do stop fussing," said Willie.

"Can't help fussing," said Basil, remembering how difficult it usually was to get Willie out of bed.

"What ARE you doing up so early?" asked Dewy.

"Where have you been?" asked Basil.

"None of your business," said Willie. And no amount of persuading or cajoling would make him tell.

6

After breakfast, and when he was sure Basil and Dewy were busy elsewhere, Willie rescued his parcel from its hiding place and carried it off into the wood.

Basil worried about Willie all morning. "I suppose he IS alright?" he kept saying.

The tenth time Basil asked the same question, Dewy didn't answer. Instead he asked a question himself.

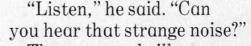

"Listen," he said. "Can you hear that strange noise?"

There was a shrill . . . hiccupping . . . kind of trill, coming from the direction of the wood.

"Must be some kind of bird," said Basil.

"Let's go and find out," said Dewy, hoping it would take Basil's mind off Willie for a while.

Dewy found the binoculars and Basil wrote a note to Willie to tell him they had gone bird watching, should he come back before they did, and then they crept into the wood.

"We're getting closer," whispered Basil. "What's funny?" he asked, as Dewy began to shake with silent laughter.

"Look there . . ." whispered Dewy, handing the binoculars to Basil. "I spy a . . . Willie-bird."

7

Willie was sitting under a bush blowing on a long wooden pipe. His cheeks were puffing in . . . and out. His chin was wobbling up . . . and down. His whiskers were quivering. His eyes were watering. He was concentrating so hard on what he was doing he didn't hear his two friends creep up behind him.

8

"BRAVO!" said Basil loudly, right in Willie's ear. Willie stopped in mid-blow. The wooden pipe sailed into the air, and so did Willie. Basil caught the pipe. Willie turned half a somersault and caught his feet in the bush behind him.

9

"That was clever of you," laughed Dewy.

"You've been spying on me," grumbled Willie, when he had untangled his feet and got over his surprise.

"Couldn't help it," said Dewy. "You can't keep the sort of noise you were making a secret for very long."

"Why didn't you want us to know what you were doing?" asked Basil.

"Because I knew you would laugh at me," said Willie. "And you did . . . didn't you."

"Only because you were funny," said Basil.

"I would like to have a pipe like that myself," said Dewy, thinking it best to change the subject quickly.

"So would I," said Basil.

"Really?" said Willie, as though he didn't quite believe them.

"Yes! Really!" said both his friends firmly.

So Willie wrote another letter, and got two more pipes. It was much more fun practising together than it had been practising alone. Willie didn't mind how much his friends laughed at him when he could laugh at them. He was glad they had discovered his secret, and so were they.

WILLIE DISAPPEARS

Basil was in a thoughtful mood. "I wonder," he said, "what is on the far side of the wood?"

"Whatever it is, it's bound to be something I wouldn't like," said Willie.

"That's silly," said Dewy. "And just to prove it we will go right now and take a look."

Willie protested. He tried to pretend his feet furt, and then that he had toothache. When that didn't work, he said he had a book he wanted to read, but Basil and Dewy had made up their minds, and so he had to go.

The wood was dark. The trees were tall and leafy, and the undergrowth thick and prickly. Presently they came upon a narrow, winding path. They followed it for a while and then suddenly, as though they were stepping through a doorway, they stepped out of the wood and into the sunshine.

"It's another world," said Willie with a gasp.

"Don't be silly," laughed Basil.

"I tell you it is . . . look, there's a castle . . . I'm going home before someone comes out and casts a spell on me." Willie turned and would have plunged back into the dark wood, but Basil caught hold of his arm.

11

"Your castle is nothing but an old ruin," he said.
"I don't like it! It's got an eye! It's looking at
me!" shivered Willie.

"That's the sun glinting on a window," scoffed Dewy.

"Come on," called Basil. "This looks interesting."

Dewy followed Basil through an ivy covered archway, and because Willie was too scared to stay by himself, he followed too. It was dark and shadowy inside.

"Whoooo aaare yoooo?" wailed a hollow voice that sent shivers darting like arrows down their backs.

13

"I told you . . . I told you," gasped Willie. Dewy spun round on his heel to tell him to be quiet.

"BASIL!" he cried in alarm. "Willie's gone. IT'S GOT WILLIE!"

Basil shook his fist at the inky shadows. "Put him back! Do you hear? PUT HIM BACK!"

"P p p p p" Dewy's voice had got stuck.

There was a sudden rush of wind and the air seemed to tremble. Dewy had never been so scared in his life. He clung to Basil and pulled him back into a dark corner.

"Did I frighten yooooo?" asked the same hollow voice, this time about an inch away from their heads. "I didn't meeeeen toooo."

"Wh wh wh what have you done with W W W Willie?" Basil was trying so hard to stop his teeth chattering.

"I haven't done anything with him," said the voice. "Please allow me to introduce myself. I am Albert Owl. I live here. This is my home."

Basil dared to look into a face with enormous, shining eyes, and was glad that he had.

"It's alright Dewy," he whispered, "it really IS an owl. We really are in a ruin."

"That's not quite correct," said the owl. "It's a home disguised to look like a ruin. Now, let's see if we can find your friend. He ran off in that direction."

They found Willie crouching against a wall with a curtain of ivy covering everything except his tail.

"I told you it would be something I didn't like," he shivered. "I'm frightened."

"There's no need to be," said Dewy, who had barely got over his own fright. "Let me introduce you to Albert Owl."

"P p p pleased t t t to m m m meet you," said Willie.

"I would be much obliged if you would step inside and take tea with me before you go home," said Albert Owl.

15

"Thank you," said Basil, "we would like that."

"I wouldn't," said Willie.

"Yes you would," said Dewy firmly. "You will like Albert when you get to know him."

And to Willie's surprise, he did.

16

THE DUCKLING

One morning, when Basil opened the front door there was a tiny duckling standing on the doorstep.

"Quack," said the duckling forlornly.

"Hallo," said Basil, taking a quick look round outside. "Are you by yourself? Where's your mother?"

Dewy came out to see who Basil was talking to.

"Hallo duckling," he said, "what are YOU doing here?"

"Quack," said the duckling sadly.

"It must be lost," said Dewy. "Stay there young 'un and we'll see if we can find your mother for you."

"Willie!" called Basil. "Come out here and look after our visitor."

Willie came to the door eating a piece of toast.

"Visitor? What visitor? I see no visitor."

"Quack," said the duckling.

"Who said that?" mumbled Willie through a mouthful of toast crumbs.

"He did," said Basil pointing to the duckling. "Now look after him . . . don't let him go away . . . we'll be back as soon as we can."

"Back? Where are you going?" asked Willie. "You're not going to leave me to look after it by myself . . . are you?"

"He's very little, and he's lost, and we're going to look for his mother. Now you be kind to him."

"You'd better hurry up and find her," called Willie as Basil and Dewy set off in opposite directions. "I might not be very good at this job." He looked the duckling over.

"Funny feathers you've got," he said.

"Quack," said the duckling.

"Is that ALL you can say?" asked Willie. "I suppose you're too young to have learnt much."

"Quack," said the duckling again. "Quack . . . quack . . ." Its little eyes were on Willie's half-eaten piece of toast.

"Oh well," sighed Willie. "I suppose I can always make myself another piece of toast when you have gone. There you are. Don't eat it all at once . . ."

He crumbled the remainder of the toast into crumbs and dropped them in front of the duckling. He stood and watched as it gobbled them up greedily.

"Glad you don't live with us," he said. "Never seen anyone eat a piece of toast that quickly before."

"He will HAVE to live with us for a while," said Basil when he and Dewy came back from their search. "Can't find the little chap's mother anywhere . . . we'll have to look after him."

"You mean, YOU will. I'm not looking after a duckling," said Willie. "I've got better things to do with MY time."

19

But the duckling had taken
a fancy to Willie, and every
where Willie went, the duckling
went too.
"Shoo . . . shoo . . . go away . . ."
grumbled Willie.
"He's adopted you," said
Basil. "He's chosen you to
be his foster-mother. You
should be very proud."

20

"Well I'm NOT," said Willie. "I don't WANT to be a duckling's mother." And to prove he meant what he said he hid under his bed. The duckling had no trouble finding HIM.

"I can't understand how it ever got itself lost in the first place," sighed Willie.

21

Nothing Willie did, or said, upset the duckling in the slightest. Willie had given him some toast so he knew Willie loved him. Every time Willie stood still, he sat on his foot and gazed up at him adoringly. Poor Willie. He didn't KNOW what to do and all Basil and Dewy did was smile.

Late that afternoon there was a knock at the door.

"If that's another duckling, don't let it in," pleaded Willie and he shut himself in the bathroom. The duckling went with him, of course.

Presently Basil tapped at the door.

"It's alright, you can come out," he called. "It's the duckling's mother. She heard he was here. She has come to take him home."

"And about time too," sighed Willie. "I'm worn out."

"Quack!" said the little duckling when it saw its real mother.

"Qua..qua..qua..quack."

Willie was forgotten. Willie was relieved.

When the ducks had finally gone and he and the badgers were having supper, Willie said dreamily, "I suppose he was rather sweet . . . I do believe I am going to miss him."

Basil and Dewy did laugh.

THE HOLE

It was sunny and hot. Willie was lying in a deck chair listening to the birds and wondering why the sky was so blue. It was the kind of afternoon when the whole world seems at rest. There was hardly a breeze to stir the leaves. There were no chores to be done and there was plenty of time to dream. Willie's eyes were just beginning to close drowsily, when the deck chair wobbled . . . ever so slightly.

"Did I imagine that, or didn't I?" thought Willie. He didn't have long to wait for an answer. The deck chair wobbled again.

"I'm getting out of here . . ." said Willie. "Something funny going on . . ." But because it was hot, he wasn't in a hurrying mood, and he was still thinking about moving when he suddenly found himself falling . . . falling . . . falling . . .

"Help," he gulped as he found himself in a dark place, and face to face with a very surprised looking rabbit.

"Where did YOU come from?" demanded the rabbit.

"From up there . . . I think," said Willie, pointing to the sky which was now a far away circle of blue.

"What's happened?" Dewy's face had appeared at the
edge of the sky. "How did you get down there?"

"He made a hole in the roof of my burrow . . . that's
what he did," complained the rabbit.

"Digging a bit close to the surface, aren't you?"
asked Basil who had also appeared at the edge of the sky.

25

The rabbit scratched his head. "I suppose I am now
you come to mention it. Should be at least six feet of
earth above me. Wait a moment and I'll measure it."

He used one of his long ears as a measuring stick.

"Definitely something wrong here," he said. "I
must have taken a wrong turning somewhere."

"I've got a map indoors," said Basil. "Come inside
and we'll have a look at it."

Basil spread the map on the kitchen table and they all
studied it carefully.

"I thought I was there . . ." said the rabbit, pointing
to a spot on the map which WAS six feet under the surface.

"Well you're not. You're in the middle of our lawn," said Basil. "You took a wrong turning, obviously."

"Most frightfully sorry," said the rabbit.

"You jolly well ought to be," said Willie. "I might have been hurt."

"So might I," said the rabbit. "You could have fallen on top of me."

"Just you make sure you don't make any more silly mistakes," said Willie. "I don't want to fall into a burrow every time I walk across the garden."

Basil rolled up the map and gave it to the rabbit.

"Take this with you," he said. HE didn't want to fall into any burrows either. HE was bigger than Willie. HE might get stuck.

"Thank you," said the rabbit. "That's most frightfully kind of you. I'll get back to my digging now."

"There's just one more thing," said Basil.

"What's that?" asked the rabbit.

"You will fill in the burrow that went wrong, won't you?"

"I'll see to it straight away," said the rabbit. And he did. And by evening it was safe to walk in the garden again.

27

A . . . A . . . SOMETHING

Dewy was weeding, Willie was pretending to be busy and Basil was on his knees in the cabbage patch.

"Someone has been eating the cabbages," said Basil.

"It wasn't me," said Willie, quickly swallowing a mouthful of peas and dropping the empty pod.

"Look . . ." said Basil. "Holes in all the leaves.
Now who would do a thing like that?"

"EEEK!" cried Willie as Basil looked up. "You've
got a . . . a . . . something . . . on your nose."

"Have I?" said Basil. "What kind of a something?"

29

"It's moving . . ." cried Willie. "It's moving . . ."

Basil wrinkled his nose and squinted along towards its tip. "It's only a little caterpillar," he said.

"Only! ONLY a caterpillar! Just let a caterpillar try to crawl on ME!" said Willie. "Just let one TRY, that's all, just let one TRY . . . I'd squash it FLAT!"

"Well don't squash this one, or my nose," said Basil and carefully returned the caterpillar to the cabbage leaf from which it had come.

"I don't think you should do that," said Dewy. "It will repay you by making more holes in the cabbages."

"It's got to eat something," said Basil.

"OOOWWW!" It was Willie again.

"What's the matter now?" asked Basil. "Did a caterpillar touch you?"

"There's one walking on me . . . take it off . . . TAKE IT OFF!"

Basil and Dewy looked. They looked carefully, but they could see nothing remotely resembling a caterpillar . . . unless . . .

"You don't mean THIS, do you?" asked Dewy, picking something green, and fat, from Willie's tummy and dangling it in front of his nose.

Willie closed his eyes tightly.

"I don't want to see it . . . take it away."

"Willie . . ." began Dewy sternly.

"I won't look . . . I WON'T!" said Willie defiantly.

"If you do you will see what . . ."

"I won't . . . I won't . . . I don't want a thing like THAT

getting near MY nose."

"Open your eyes!" ordered Basil.

"Shan't! Won't! Can't! Not going to!"

"If you don't I'll put it back," threatened Dewy.

"You wouldn't dare!" said Willie, but just to make sure he quickly opened one eye and peeped. He closed it again, just as quickly, when he saw Dewy was still dangling the fat . . . green . . . horrible . . . THING . . . in front of his nose.

"We're wasting our time," said Dewy. "I'm going indoors to get supper. I'm taking THIS with me. Willie will have to come indoors too if he wants to see what it is."

"I don't WANT to see it," said Willie and he stood right where he was, with his eyes tightly closed until he was sure Dewy and Basil and the THING had gone.

When it felt safe he opened his eyes and carefully
stepped out of the cabbage patch. He was going as far away
from cabbage eating caterpillars as he could. How was he
to know cabbages weren't the only thing caterpillars lived
on. But what Willie didn't see, Willie didn't worry about.

32

He sat beside the pond until he felt hungry and then he
went to the back door. He knocked loudly.

"YOU don't have to knock," said Basil when he saw who
it was. "YOU live here. YOU can come straight in."

"Not with THAT thing in the house," said Willie.

Dewy appeared beside Basil and held up a jar.

"It's in here," he said.

"Keep it away from me," said Willie, with a shudder.

"It won't hurt you," said Dewy, staring at Willie's head and trying not to giggle. "Here . . . read the label."

Very, very cautiously, Willie leant towards the jar.

"Go on . . . read what it says," urged Basil.

"Dangerous . . ." read Willie with a sharp intake of breath. "Found crawling on Willie. An empty pea pod."

There was a long, long, silence as Willie looked at the empty pea pod, and Dewy and Basil looked at the striped caterpillar looping the loop over Willie's head.

"Well, it looked like a giant caterpillar," said Willie at last. "How was I to know it wasn't?"

"All you had to do was open your eyes," said Dewy.

"You should have told me what it was," said Willie.

"We don't have to tell you everything," laughed Dewy, as Basil slipped behind Willie and secretly removed the real caterpillar and put it on a leafy plant. That was something else they wouldn't tell Willie about. He would have made far too much fuss.

TREASURE

Willie had been down the lane to see if there were any letters in the letterbox. He was on his way back when he heard a rustling in the undergrowth. There was something, or someone, throwing leaves and twigs into the air.

"Who's there?" he called, getting ready to run.

"It's me," answered Jake Squirrel from the very centre of a leafy whirlwind.

"What are you doing?" asked Willie.

"What do you think I'm doing? Can't you see I'm looking for something?" Jake Squirrel had more than a hint of crossness in his voice. "Any more silly questions?"

"There's no need to be rude," said Willie. "It's just that you're usually up there," he pointed to the branches above his head, ". . . and so I wondered what you were doing down there."

"Go away and leave me alone," said Jake. "I'm too busy to waste time talking to you."

"Very well," said Willie and continued thoughtfully on his way. 'If Jake Squirrel is looking for something . . .' he thought, 'he must have lost something.' He turned about and went back to where Jake was turning over leaves.

"What have you lost?"
asked Willie politely.
Jake didn't like being
interrupted and shook his fist.
"I've lost my treasure . . .
that's what I've done . . . I've
lost my treasure . . . I dropped
it when I was up there . . . and
now it's down here . . . and I
CAN'T FIND IT!"

36

"TREASURE!" exclaimed Willie.

He dived into the leaves at Jake's feet and began to throw them into the air. If there was treasure to be found, he was joining in the search.

"And what do you think YOU'RE doing? asked Jake Squirrel, yanking him to his feet.

"Searching for the treasure of course."

"As long as you remember it's MY treasure when it's found."

"Of course I will," said Willie. "But if it's me who finds it perhaps you'll see your way clear to giving me just a teeny, weeny, little bit of it, for myself."

"I might, and then again, I might not," said Jake. "Now get searching. I'm hungry."

Willie couldn't see what being hungry had to do with finding treasure but he didn't think it wise to ask any more questions at that precise moment.

He'd been throwing leaves around for ten minutes before it occurred to him he didn't know what he was looking for.

"Er, um," he coughed shyly, as though he didn't really want to bother Jake.

"What is it?" asked Jake crossly.

"Er . . . er . . . what does your treasure look like?"

"Brown and round and fat."

"Oh . . ." said Willie. "You didn't mean to say sparkly and shiny and golden did you?" Sparkly and shiny and golden seemed a much better description of a treasure to him.

"No, I didn't," said Jake. "Now, are you helping me or not?"

"Of course I am," said Willie, though he wasn't quite so sure that he wanted to now. He was almost relieved when Jake threw a bundle of leaves into the air and shouted,

"I'VE FOUND IT!"

"Let me see it," cried Willie eagerly. When he saw what Jake was holding he could hardly believe his eyes.

"But THAT'S a NUT!" he said, "a plain, ordinary, common-or-woodland NUT!"

"It might seem plain and ordinary to you," said Jake Squirrel, "but it's treasure to ME. I've been saving it for months. It's the most beautiful nut I have ever found and I am going to eat it on my birthday."

"I would never have stopped to help if I'd known what it was I was searching for," grumbled Willie. "When you said treasure, I thought you meant real treasure."

"Moles are very hard to understand sometimes," said Jake Squirrel.

"So are squirrels!" retorted Willie crossly.

Later that day Willie took out his own treasures, which he kept hidden in a box at the bottom of his wardrobe, and looked at them lovingly, one by one.

"I suppose MY treasures are only treasures to ME," he said. "I wouldn't like to lose any of mine either."

40

A PROBLEM

The Ash Lodge pond stretches between the trees as
though it is part of a winding river. It is possible to
walk all round it of course, but more and more often, the
badgers and Willie found themselves ferrying their friends
across the middle of it, on their raft.

If someone had an errand to do on the far side of the pond, they would call in at Ash Lodge, and drop hints about how much time it would save if only they could go across the pond, instead of round it.

"This is such a useful shortcut," said Hannah Hedgehog as Basil ferried her across one morning.

"I can see that it must be," said Basil, trying not to sigh as Hannah settled herself comfortably. He had been sitting comfortably himself, making plans for the day, when Hannah had called.

"You've no idea how long it used to take me to walk all the way round the edge of the pond," she said brightly. "I've got rather short legs you know. I was always arriving too late for EVERYTHING."

"You won't forget to keep a look out and come across for me when I return, will you?" she said as she stepped ashore.

There were three dormice lazing on the bank.

"Knew you'd come, sooner or later," they said, "didn't feel like walking." They scrambled onto the raft without so much as a by-your-leave and lay on their backs with their tails trailing in the water while Basil did all the work.

"Thanks for the lift Baz!" they called cheekily as they hopped off on the opposite bank.

"Oh dear," sighed Basil when he got back to the house. "I feel tired already and the day has hardly begun. Perhaps we should sink the raft and put a stop to all this ferrying backwards and forwards."

"We couldn't possibly do that!" exclaimed Dewy.

"Our friends rely on us."

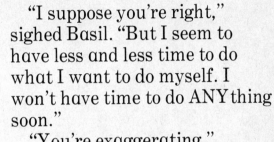

"I suppose you're right," sighed Basil. "But I seem to have less and less time to do what I want to do myself. I won't have time to do ANYthing soon."

"You're exaggerating," laughed Dewy. But when he had to put his book down in the middle of an exciting chapter to go across the pond and bring Hannah back, HE sighed too, and said, "I wish there was another way of crossing the pond."

"Pity there isn't a bridge," said Willie.

"Willie, you're a genius!" cried Basil. "We'll build a bridge."

"Who? US?" asked Willie disbelievingly.

"Do you think we could?" asked Dewy.

"I don't see why not," said Basil.

They asked Otley Otter to help them. He was used to
working under water. As they rolled the logs into the pond
he roped them together. When there were enough to stretch
right across the pond he anchored them firmly, so that they
would not float away. They all agreed they could never
have made the bridge without his help.

"How would YOU like to be the first to use the new bridge?" Basil asked Otley.

"Well," said Otley, "as you know, I usually swim across the pond, but just this once I think I WILL walk."

"I announce this bridge officially open," he said as everyone followed him across.

45

Otley promised to keep a special watch on the underneath side of the bridge to see that none of the logs broke loose and he also promised to rescue anyone who was foolish enough to fall off the bridge and into the pond.

"I'll be special bridge-keeper and life guard," he laughed.

For the next few days the bridge was as busy as a town street. Everyone found a good reason for going across at least twice a day and if they hadn't a real reason they made one up. Willie was the one who fell off it, of course. Basil said he would have been MORE surprised if Willie hadn't fallen off. The splash he made as he fell in sent the water bouncing in waves against the banks. It made the logs rock dizzily and frightened all the ducks. Otley managed to catch hold of him before he swallowed too much pondweed.

"How did you manage to do that?" asked Otley as he towed Willie ashore.

"Do what?" spluttered Willie.

"Fall off a perfectly safe bridge."

"I was looking at my reflection," mumbled Willie, "I . . . er . . . sort of . . . er . . . over balanced."